# Dotty Lends a Dream

# DOtty Lends a Dream

written and illustrated by

CATHERINE MARY BROWN

WHITE COTTON CLOUDS RACED IN SUCH
A SPLENDID HURRY, THEIR JOURNEY NEVER
ENDING. PUSHED ALONG BY THE GENTLE
BREEZE, RACING TUFTS OF DELIGHTFUL
FLUFFINESS.

NESTLED AMONG THOSE MOVING VELVETY CLOUDS, THE DAZZLING YELLOW SUN GLOWED, ITS BRIGHTNESS GIVING WARMTH TO ALL IT TOUCHED.

SUCH COMFORTING HAPPINESS COVERING THE LAND BELOW.

ROLLING SLOPING FIELDS LAY BENEATH, A MEADOW FULL OF THE RICHES OF LUSCIOUS GREEN GRASSES AND THE FINEST FLOWERS IN ALL THE COLOURS OF THE RAINBOW.

TREES, SO ELEGANTLY TALL, PROUDLY STAND IN THE PASTURES, THEIR STRONG STURDY BRANCHES GIVING BIRDS A SAFE PLACE TO SIT AND SING, MAJESTIC MUSICAL SOUNDS FILLING THE AIR ALL AROUND.

OH, HOW THE BUTTERFLIES DANCED, FLOATING AND SWAYING TO THE WONDERFUL SOUND. THEIR COLOURS MERGING AS ONE. SO VERY GRACEFUL; A DELIGHT TO BEHOLD.

BUT WE ALL KNOW THAT DAY DOES IN FACT TURN TO NIGHT; THE LAND AND THE SKY BOTH CHANGE, NEW COLOURS, SHIMMERING SILVERS EMERGE.

AS THE MOON RISES, RESTS HIGH IN THE SKY, ALL THE CREATURES KNOW THAT NOW IT IS TIME TO SLEEP. ALL TUCKED IN AND SO VERY, VERY COMFORTABLE READY FOR THE DREAMS THAT WILL FOLLOW.

BUT LOOK, JUST THERE, SITTING IN THE LUSH GRASS, THERE SEEMS TO BE ONE LITTLE CREATURE THAT IS NOT QUITE READY TO GO TO BED.

'CAN YOU SEE?'

JUST WAITING WITH THE SWAYING LUSH GRASS ALL AROUND, WAITING IN A VERY PATIENT KIND OF WAY TO MEET THE MOON.

ALL IS COVERED BY A BLANKET OF WARMTH AND ALL BUT ONE HAS CLOSED THEIR TIRED EYES DREAMING OF THE DAY'S EVENTS.

YES, ALL BUT ONE...

THIS LITTLE CREATURE WAS NOT IN THE MOOD TO SLEEP; IT DID NOT FEEL TIRED, NO, NOT ONE LITTLE BIT!

'CAN YOU TELL WHAT KIND OF CREATURE IT IS?'

WELL, IT JUST SO HAPPENS TO BE ONE PATIENT LITTLE DINOSAUR AND ITS NAME WAS DOTTY, WAITING IN SUCH AN EXCITED WAY!

YOU MUST UNDERSTAND WHY THIS LITTLE DINOSAUR WAS FILLED WITH ENTHUSIASM, WHY IT WAS BURSTING ALMOST WITH ANTICIPATION TO TELL THE SHIMMERING MOON SOMETHING ONLY IT COULD HEAR.

THAT WAS THE BEST PART OF BEING A MOON - IT MEANT THAT ALL THE CREATURES OF THE LAND COULD SHARE, LEND THEIR DREAMS.

SO, DOTTY TOOK WHAT MIGHT BE THE BIGGEST OF BREATHS THAT ANY OTHER CREATURE HAD EVER HAD.

THIS WAS ONE VERY EXCITED DINOSAUR AND SO AS SHE TOOK IN ALL THE AIR UNTIL SHE THOUGHT THAT HER LUNGS WERE GOING TO POP, THEN, SHE BEGAN TO LEND HER DREAM TO THE PATIENTLY LISTENING MOON...

WITH THAT BIG BREATH, SHE BEGAN TO SHARE WHAT WAS CAUSING HER GIDDINESS, HER JUBILATION. THE VERY THING THAT SHE DREAMT OF WAS BUILDING THE BIGGEST OF ROCKETS THAT HAD EVER BEEN MADE. NOT ONE CREATURE WOULD HAVE SEEN SUCH A THING, NO, NOT AT ALL!

DOTTY THE LITTLE DINOSAUR TOLD THE PATIENTLY LISTENING
MOON THAT HER ROCKET, WELL, IT WOULD HAVE

A LONG RECTANGLE BODY,

A TRIANGLE-SHAPED TOP,

A ROUND WINDOW.

OH YES, INDEED!

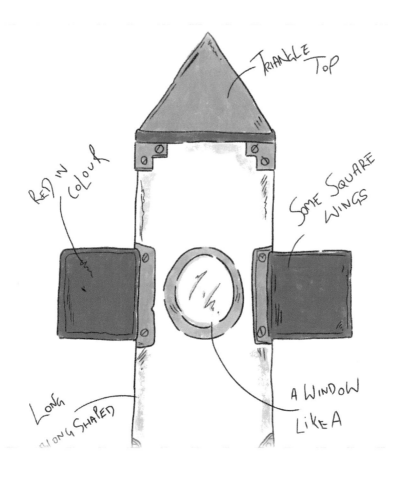

THERE WOULD BE BRIGHT RED SQUARE WINGS AND ANOTHER AT THE END OF THE RECTANGLE BODY SO THAT SHE COULD BLAST HER WAY TO JOLLY JUPITER. WHIZZ TO MERRY MARS.

FROM THE ROUND WINDOW, SHE WOULD SEE THOSE LUSCIOUS GREEN FIELDS, THE MEADOW OF FLOWERS AND THE TALL PROUD TREES THAT STOOD TO ATTENTION IN A LONG ROW.

OH YES, UP, AROUND, ON QUITE POSSIBLY ONE VERY ADVENTUROUS TRIP INDEED.

JUST TO BE NEAR THE SPARKLING STARS, SO CLOSE THAT
A CREATURE MIGHT ALMOST BE ABLE TO TOUCH THEIR
PRETTINESS.

AND STILL, THE SILENT PATIENTLY LISTENING MOON SMILED
DOWN AT THE LITTLE DINOSAUR.

DOTTY WAS SO ELATED AND FOCUSED, THINKING HOW SHE
MIGHT ZIP AND WHIZZ THROUGH THE SKIES ABOVE, THAT SHE
DID NOT SEEM TO NOTICE THAT NOW THE MOON, WELL, IT WAS
YAWNING, QUITE POSSIBLY THE BIGGEST SLEEPINESS OF YAWNS
YOU MIGHT EVER SEE!

SHE HAD NOT NOTICED THE CHANGING SKIES, THAT NIGHT WAS
IN FACT TURNING ONCE AGAIN TO DAY. IT WAS TIME NOW FOR
THE BEAUTIFUL DAZZLING YELLOW SUN TO RISE ONCE MORE
AND TIME TO BID FAREWELL TO THE SHIMMERING MOON.

YES, NOW IT WAS TIME TO REST...

GENTLY, THE MOON BRUSHED THE LITTLE DINOSAUR'S SOFT
ROSY CHEEK, KISSING IT SO VERY TENDERLY.

FOR YOU MUST UNDERSTAND NOW WAS THE TIME FOR IT TO
DREAM AND SO AS IT WHISPERED GOOD NIGHT, IT ASKED
DOTTY A VERY IMPORTANT QUESTION...

'DOTTY, COULD YOU POSSIBLY LEND ME ANOTHER DREAM?

I WOULD LOVE TO HEAR ABOUT MORE ADVENTURES IN YOUR
SUPER-POWERED ROCKET MACHINE. WHERE MIGHT YOU TRAVEL
NEXT?' THE MOON WONDERED.

DOTTY STRETCHED; OH, HOW HAPPY WAS SHE THAT THE MOON, A SHIMMERING SILVER COLOUR, HAD TAKEN THE TIME TO LISTEN TO THE LITTLE DINOSAUR'S THOUGHTS AND DELIGHTS.

IT HAD SMILED FROM HIGH IN THE SKY AND EMBRACED, CUDDLED THE VERY IDEA OF SUCH A WONDERFUL DREAM, IN FACT, IT WANTED TO LISTEN ONCE MORE TO WHERE SHE MIGHT TRAVEL, BLASTING THROUGH THE UNIVERSE WITH THE STARS GLISTENING ALL AROUND AND AROUND IN THE MIDNIGHT AIR.

WITH A VERY GOOD WARM FEELING IN HER TUMMY, SHE
SKIPPED OFF IMAGINING OTHER JOURNEYS SHE MIGHT TAKE
IN HER WONDERFUL CREATION, BLASTING, WHIZZING SO VERY
MERRILY AROUND THE WORLD BELOW!

TO DREAM THOUGHTS IS A WONDROUS THING BUT IF YOU
SHARE THEM WITH A FRIEND SO THAT THEY CAN ENJOY YOUR
ADVENTURE WITH YOU, IT MAKES EVERYTHING SO VERY SPECIAL.

SUCH A BEAUTIFUL GIFT FROM ONE CREATURE TO ANOTHER.

'CAN YOU REMEMBER ANY
DELIGHTFUL DREAMS
YOU MIGHT WISH TO SHARE?'

CPSIA information can be obtained
at www.ICGtesting.com
Printed in the USA
BVHW011133140223
658470BV00020B/15

* 9 7 8 1 8 0 2 2 7 7 9 6 8 *